W9-AMN-757

This book belongs to

EAU CLAIRE DISTRICT LIBRARY

TM & © 1950, 1951, 1958, renewed 1977, 1979, 1986 by Dr. Seuss Enterprises, L.P.
All rights reserved under International and Pan-American Copyright Conventions.
Published in the United States by Random House, Inc., New York,
and simultaneously in Canada by Random House of Canada Limited, Toronto.

Previously published by Random House, Inc., in 1958 in *Yertle the Turtle and Other Stories*.

http://www.randomhouse.com/

Library of Congress Cataloging-in-Publication Data
Seuss, Dr.
The big brag / by Dr. Seuss.
p. cm. — "A Little Dipper book." SUMMARY: A rhyming story in which
a rabbit and a bear argue about which one of them is the best, until a worm reveals the truth.
ISBN 0-679-89149-8 (trade). — ISBN 0-679-99149-2 (lib. bdg.)
[1. Rabbits—Fiction. 2. Bears—Fiction. 3. Worms—Fiction. 4. Pride and vanity—Fiction.
5. Stories in rhyme.] I. Title. PZ8.3.G276Bi 1998 [E]—dc21 97-32463

Printed in the United States of America 10 9 8 7 6 5 4 3 2 1

LITTLE DIPPER is a trademark of Random House, Inc.

The Big Brag

By Dr. Seuss

* A Little Dipper™ Book *

RANDOM HOUSE 🏠 NEW YORK

BPT 10-29-98 #7.99

EAU CLAIRE DISTRICT LIBRARY

The rabbit felt mighty important that day
On top of the hill in the sun where he lay.
He felt SO important up there on that hill
That he started in bragging, as animals will,
And he boasted out loud, as he threw out his chest,
"Of all of the beasts in the world, I'm the best!
On land, and on sea…even up in the sky
No animal lives who is better than I!"

"What's *that?*" growled a voice that was terribly gruff.
"Now why do you say such ridiculous stuff?"
The rabbit looked down and he saw a big bear.
"*I'm* best of the beasts," said the bear. "And so there!"

"You're not!" snapped the rabbit. "I'm better than you!"
"Pooh!" the bear snorted. "Again I say Pooh!
You talk mighty big, Mr. Rabbit. That's true.
But how can you prove it? **Just what can you DO?**"

"Hmmmm…" thought the rabbit,
"Now what CAN I do…?"
He thought and he thought. Then he finally said,
"Mr. Bear, do you see these two ears on my head?
My ears are so keen and so sharp and so fine
No ears in the world can hear further than mine!"

"Humpf!" the bear grunted. He looked at each ear.
"You *say* they are good," said the bear with a sneer,
"But how do *I* know just how far they can hear?"

"I'll prove," said the rabbit, "my ears are the best.
You sit there and watch me. I'll prove it by test."
Then he stiffened his ears till they both stood up high
And pointed straight up at the blue of the sky.
He stretched his ears open as wide as he could.
"Shhh! I am listening!" he said as he stood.
He listened so hard that he started to sweat
And the fur on his ears and his forehead got wet.

For seven long minutes he stood. Then he stirred
And he said to the bear, "Do you know what I heard?
Do you see that far mountain…? It's ninety miles off.
There's a fly on that mountain. I just heard him cough!
Now the cough of a fly, sir, is quite hard to hear
When he's ninety miles off. But I heard it quite clear.
So you see," bragged the rabbit, "it's perfectly true
That my ears are the best, so I'm better than you!"

The bear, for a moment, just sulked as he sat
For he knew that *his* ears couldn't hear things like *that*.
"This rabbit," he thought, "made a fool out of me.
Now *I've* got to prove that I'm better than he."
So he said to the rabbit, "You hear pretty well.
You can hear ninety miles. *But how far can you smell?*
I'm the greatest of smellers," he bragged. "See my nose?
This nose on my face is the finest that grows.
My nose can smell *anything*, both far and near.
With my nose I can smell twice as far as you hear!"

"You can't!" snapped the rabbit.
"I can!" growled the bear.
And he stuck his big nose
'way up high in the air.

He wiggled that nose and he sniffed and he snuffed.
He waggled that nose and he whiffed and he whuffed.
For more than ten minutes he snaff and he snuff.
Then he said to the rabbit, "I've smelled far enough."

"All right," said the rabbit. "Come on now and tell
Exactly how far is the smell that you smell?"

"Oh, I'm smelling a *very* far smell," said the bear.
"Away past that fly on that mountain out there.
I'm smelling past many great mountains beyond
Six hundred miles more to the edge of a pond."

EAU CLAIRE DISTRICT LIBRARY

"And 'way, 'way out there, by the pond you can't see,
Is a very small farm. On the farm is a tree.
On the tree is a branch. On the branch is a nest,
A very small nest where two tiny eggs rest.
Two hummingbird eggs! Only half an inch long!
But my nose," said the bear, "is so wonderfully strong,
My nose is so good that I smelled without fail
That the egg on the left is a little bit stale!
And *that* is a thing that no rabbit can do.
So you see," the bear boasted, "I'm better than you!
My smeller's so keen that it just can't be beat…"

"**What's that?**" called a voice
From 'way down by his feet.
The bear and the rabbit looked down at the sound,
And they saw an old worm crawling out of the ground.

"Now, boys," said the worm, "you've been bragging a lot.
You both think you're great. But *I* think you are not.
You're not half as good as a fellow like me.
You hear and you smell. *But how far can you SEE?*
Now, *I'm* here to prove to you big boasting guys
That your nose and your ears aren't as good as my eyes!"

And the little old worm cocked his head to one side
And he opened his eyes and he opened them wide.
And they looked far away with a strange sort of stare.
As if they were burning two holes in the air.
The eyes of that worm almost popped from his head.
He stared half an hour till his eyelids got red.
"That's enough!" growled the bear.
"Tell the rabbit and me
How far did you look and just what did you see?"

"Well, boys," the worm answered, "that look that I took
Was a look that looked farther than *you'll* ever look!
I looked 'cross the ocean, 'way out to Japan.
For I can see farther than anyone can.
There's no one on earth who has eyesight that's finer.
I looked past Japan. Then I looked across China.
I looked across Egypt; then took a quick glance
Across the two countries of Holland and France.
Then I looked across England and, also, Brazil.
But I didn't stop there. I looked much farther still.

"And I kept right on looking and looking until
I'd looked 'round the world and right back to this hill!
And I saw on this hill, since my eyesight's so keen,
The two biggest fools that have ever been seen!
And the fools that I saw were none other than you,
Who seem to have nothing else better to do
Than sit here and argue who's better than who!"

Then the little old worm gave his head a small jerk
And he dived in his hole and went back to his work.

EAU CLAIRE DISTRICT LIBRARY